Pick Up
The Pieces

Ric Perrott

Mirelune Press

First published by Mirelune Press 2025

www.mirelune.com

This story is entirely a work of fiction. The names, characters and incidents portrayed in it are the work of the author's imagination. Any resemblance to actual persons, living or dead, events or localities is entirely coincidental.

First Paperback Edition

ISBN: 979-8-9995624-8-7 (Paperback)

Cover Design: 100covers

Dice Image by: Cristina Gaidau for Vecteezy.com

v2,3

For Matt, Marisha, Laura, Travis, Ashley, Taliesin, Liam, Sam and everyone at Critical Role. Thanks for the games.

Pick Up The Pieces

Roll For Initiative

The campaign binders fill the top shelf of my study. *Vol. 1: The Ashen Prophecy*. *Vol. 4: The Sundered Throne*. Seven volumes, the last one still half-empty. My fingers run along their worn spines, Eldyrane's complete history recorded in careful script. My hands shake more now, and my wedding ring jostles around when I reach up to straighten them. A task that once took a few minutes now demands the better part of the morning. The cancer has taken my strength, my weight, and my future. But these stories remain unaffected.

Weeks, the doctor says, maybe a month. Time to organize my affairs, but not to finish what matters. The cardigan comes up around my shoulders. To think this sweater used to feel tight, now it hangs on me like a straitjacket.

My office is filled with the scents of the medicinal teas Ellen insists will help and the musty perfume of books I've collected over decades. The morning light refracts through the stained glass, illuminating the room with colors that dance like the ethereal sprites I once described to the guys.

The dice rattle against one another as I open the

drawer. It's a familiar, hollow sound that once signaled possibility. Now they sound like bones.

"And so the Silver Conclave falls," I murmur to the empty room. "Its towers crumble into the Endless Sea as Lord Vathek's laughter echoes across the waves."

No one's listening. I haven't spoken to the guys in months. When Ellen posted about my diagnosis, they sent messages, awkward, well-meaning things about thoughts and prayers. Then silence. No blame rests with them. What do you say to a dying dungeon master? You can't cast Regenerate on a pancreas in real life.

The simple act of standing has drained my meager energy, and I sink into the recliner. The pill bottles on my side table are stacked in rows. I've started naming them after minor villains from our campaign.

The final binder sits on the desk, notes half-finished. In our last session, they'd discovered the ancient mechanism beneath the City of Brass. Seraphiel's redemption arc is sketched out but unearned. Brian might have even tried to pickpocket another fire elemental, a glorious disaster I'd never get to preside over. Ten years, and I'd left them stranded in the middle of the last act.

With the binder open, I thumb through my notes. The ultimate confrontation, the revelation about Seraphiel's true lineage, the choice that would determine the fate of Eldyrane. All outlined in my scrawling hand, never to be voiced. A few months ago, when I had the foolish thought of continuing one day, I'd even dictated them to Ellen in the living room.

"Some storyteller." The words are self-inflicted barbs. "Couldn't even finish the damn thing."

OUTSIDE, ELLEN'S CAR PULLS INTO THE driveway. She's been running mysterious errands for the last few days. Probably more appointments to schedule, more papers to sign.

Forty-three years of marriage, and she still surprises me. When the first mention of this *online role-playing thing* came up, I'd braced for the eye-roll, the gentle suggestion that perhaps a man my age should find more...appropriate hobbies. Instead, she'd simply asked, "Does it make you happy?" When I nodded, she'd said, "Then I hope they appreciate what they're getting."

She never joined us—she respected that this was my space—but she became part of our world anyway. Bringing me tea during late sessions when my voice grew hoarse. Listening to my eager recaps over breakfast, asking thoughtful questions about character motivations and plot developments. She understood what my colleagues never did—that this was about connection, not escapism.

When the diagnosis came, her backbone straightened in ways mine couldn't. As I retreated, she advanced. While I pushed people away, she held our world together. She fielded the worried calls and managed the appointments that overwhelmed me, even kept the guys updated when pride kept me from admitting how bad things had gotten.

For decades of my life, I've analyzed literature, dissecting the great love stories of fiction. But none of them prepared me for the quiet heroism of a woman who holds your hand through chemo and still asks about your imaginary worlds. Who sees the man you are behind the illness and the man you are behind the screen, and loves both versions equally.

The binder goes back on the desk. The characters

we all created together deserved better than to be abandoned in narrative limbo. But then, stories rarely end when and how we want them to.

I've been chronicling imaginary worlds for decades, but never scripted my own departure. That's an irony I wasn't expecting: the dungeon master, done in by poor planning.

The doorbell chimes.

My head tilts, listening for Ellen's footsteps in the hallway. Nothing. Probably in the garden, lost in her pruning meditation.

"Coming," I call out, my voice a thin thread of what it once was.

Could be the pharmacy delivery Ellen mentioned. Shuffling to the door in faded slippers, one hand braces against the wall for balance. The effort feels monumental, but the feeling of being waited on has grown tiresome.

The knob turns, the door swings open, and the world gets woozy like when the chemo first kicks in.

Three men stand on my porch. Unknown to my eyes perhaps, but not to my heart. I recognize them straightaway.

The stocky one can't keep still, a restless energy in how he shifts from foot to foot. He runs a hand through thinning hair, a gesture I've heard a hundred times in my headphones as a nervous tic before a risky dice roll.

Brian. Has to be.

The tall, composed Korean man with impeccable posture and a neutral expression, holding a leather messenger bag. His eyes assess me with clinical precision.

Kevin. Without question.

And off to the side, a pale, rail-thin figure with

hunched shoulders and a gaze fixed firmly on my welcome mat, fingers twitching at his sides.

Nate. Definitely.

"Hey, Walt," Brian says, his voice the same boisterous tone that's announced countless critical hits and catastrophic failures. The same voice that once declared, "I seduce the Gelatinous Cube," and tried to perform a Waltz of Seduction that left us all in stitches for ten minutes straight.

Kevin gives a single, precise nod. Economical in movement as he is in words.

Nate remains silent, a slight tremor visible in his hands.

My mouth opens, but no sound comes out, only a dry click of the tongue. My breath catches. They've traveled across states, left their lives behind, crossed the divide between digital and physical, for what? For a dying old man who couldn't finish his story?

"You came," the words catch in my throat.

My vision swims, blurring at the edges. Fingers clutch the doorframe, anchoring me to the real. After a decade, the very adventurers I'd challenged with impossible odds, showered with legendary rewards, and secretly cherished stand before me, flesh and blood on my worn welcome mat.

My eyes flick from Brian's nervous energy to Kevin's stillness to Nate's downcast gaze. *Sir Gallant. Brother Iriel. Seraphiel.* The knights of fallen empires and saviors of forgotten kings, here to continue the story.

"We couldn't miss the finale," Brian says, attempting lightness but betrayed by the thickness in his voice.

Behind them, Ellen stands on the porch, the smile I love transforming her face. Not errands. Arrangements. For them. For me.

The knot in my chest loosens, a pressure I didn't know was there until it was gone. It's a feeling so unfamiliar, so sharp after months of dull ache, that for a moment it registers as pain rather than hope. They didn't come for Eldyrane. They came for me.

Gesturing inside, I move backward, my hand remaining on the wall.

"I'll set everything up in Walt's office," Ellen says, slipping inside as if this extraordinary collision of worlds is the most natural thing imaginable.

The three of them file past me, an awkward procession of strangers who know me better than my neighbors of twenty years.

The forum post that started it all comes to mind. Buried on page four of "Looking for Group," sandwiched between minmaxers seeking optimization tips and casual players wanting beer-and-pretzels dungeon crawls. Kevin's post was different: "Seeking long-term campaign focused on character development and collaborative storytelling. DM with experience preferred. Serious inquiries only." Clinical, precise, but something in his words captured me.

Brian had responded first with his typical enthusiasm: "Count me in! I've got a rogue concept that'll either save the party or get everyone killed... probably both!" Then, two days later, Nate wrote a single line: "Would be interested if the group is patient with newer players." Even through text, I felt his uncertainty.

Reaching out tested my courage. Fifty-three years old, a tenured professor, trying to play with strangers online? I'd played on the table for twenty years at that point, but something about that trio called to me. Kevin's hunger for depth, Brian's infectious energy, Nate's silent hope. They were looking for more than a game, something I'd been searching for too, without knowing it.

Our first session was supposed to be a one-shot. A trial run. A simple campaign I'd constructed with few surprises, but when Nate's paladin made his first stand and gave a speech that silenced the party for five minutes; when Brian's rogue surprised us all with ill-advised courage and unexpected wisdom; when Kevin's composed cleric kept the party alive, I knew we'd found something rare. A bond had begun.

And now, ten years later, they're here. Walking in my hallway as if they belong here, because they do. Brian moves with a slight bounce that matches his online energy. Kevin steps with precise economy. Nate glides as if he's trying not to disturb the surrounding air.

"So," Brian clears his throat, hands fidgeting with a twenty-sided die he's pulled from his pocket. "Ready to pick up where we left off, Dungeon Master? The City of Brass awaits its fate." His smile wavers between hope and uncertainty.

"I don't think that—" My protest dies as we enter my office and Ellen's handiwork becomes clear. My recliner is at the head of a card table, with three folding chairs arranged around it, like a council meeting.

"We thought we could just talk," Kevin interrupts. From his messenger bag, he pulls out a leather portfolio and opens it. Inside, his character sheet—the same one he's been using for six years—sits protected in a plastic sleeve with meticulous notes written in blue ink.

"About old times," Brian adds, setting a shoebox on the table and removing the lid. Inside, dozens of miniatures nestle in foam dividers. He picks up a painted figure with a blue cloak. "Remember when Sir Gallant accidentally started that cult in Winterhaven?"

A smile tugs at my lips despite myself. "The Temple of the Azure Blade. You convinced them you were a demigod."

"Three natural twenties in a row." He places the miniature on the table with reverence.

Nate steps forward, still not meeting my eyes directly. He unwraps something from a cloth bundle— a handmade dice bag, embroidered with a silver tree. When he loosens the drawstring, a set of opalescent dice spills into his palm.

"I've only ever used these for Seraphiel," he says, his voice so reserved I have to lean forward. "But I thought...the party could use them today."

Ellen comes into the office with a tray of mugs and a plate of cookies, and I pull her aside, behind my desk. She sets the tray down without ceremony.

"You did this?" I whisper, my voice rough with emotion, gesturing at the gathering of unlikely pilgrims in my office.

Her eyes crinkle at the corners as she pours coffee into a mug. "Of course I did. You think I'd let you leave a story unfinished?" She straightens the stack of napkins. "These men have been in our home for years. Just never in person, that's all."

There's a practicality in her love that undoes me. She leans in and presses her lips to my forehead, her hand gentle against my face.

"Now, Mister Dungeon Master." She brushes my shoulders. "Go finish your story." She picks up the tray and brings it to the table.

Unable to speak past the tightness in my throat, I just nod. The weight of everything left unsaid, this brotherhood forged through make-believe. It all wells inside of me. I choke down the emotion, open the bottom drawer of my desk, and pull out my old DM screen, cardboard worn at the corners. A yellow sticky note still clings to one panel: *Secret trapdoor: DC 18.* Beneath it, three manuscript boxes sit in darkness, novels that were finished years ago, complete stories that never found their way to publishers' desks.

They were written in isolation, with every sentence crafted alone in this office. Careful prose, plotted arcs, characters I thought I understood completely. But they felt hollow on the page, static things that never breathed. Reading them back was like examining pressed flowers—beautiful to observe, but devoid of life.

When I flip through the Eldyrane binders, my campaign outlines, adorned with Kevin's meticulous notes, Nate's literary soliloquies, and Brian's action-hero quips scribbled in the margins, it breathes. It's more real than anything I'd written alone. All those years teaching Joyce and Hemingway... and the only story I ever truly mastered was the one I didn't write at all. It's the one I *played* with strangers on the internet. Every session with them taught me what my novels couldn't: the best stories aren't written alone in silence. They're discovered, one roll at a time.

My hands tremble as the screen unfolds and sets upright before me. Behind this flimsy barricade, a thousand characters have been born into our shared world; perhaps there are more to come.

They're watching me with expressions I've only ever had to imagine before. My trembling hand reaches for the worn binder: Volume Seven, our final chapter.

"The last time we played," I begin, my voice a whisper, "you had stumbled upon the ancient mechanism beneath the City of Brass."

Their faces are expectant, patient, and kind. I breathe, and something shifts inside me. The voice that emerges isn't the frail one that's become my daily companion. It's deeper, richer, what my students used to call my King Lear narrator.

"The brass gears turn with agonizing slowness," I intone, "revealing a chamber that has not seen light in thousands of years…"

And just like that, we're back. The story was never over. It was merely slumbering.

The session begins with confidence, but it doesn't last. Midway through describing the mythic chamber beneath the city, my voice catches. The tremor in my hands rattles the dice, and they tumble, scattering across the table. My wedding ring follows.

"Damn it," I mutter, trying to collect them. My fingers won't cooperate. The medication makes me clumsy, disconnected from my intentions.

Brian reaches over, grabs my ring, and places it gently before me. No jokes. No teasing. His expression remains neutral, but it's clear what he's hiding.

They're watching me with that stare, the one everyone gives the terminally ill. Part pity, part fear, as if my condition might be contagious.

"I'm sorry," I say, my voice weak. "I'm not what I was."

The silence stretches. The words of my notes swim in front of me. The elaborate description of the crystalline pillars and timeworn runes blurs into meaningless squiggles. Ten years of storytelling, and I can't remember what comes next.

A different tightness takes hold now, one that the pills can't help. The fear of a storyteller who has lost his words. My breath, already shallow, catches on the thought: what if this is how they remember me? Not with a stride, but with a stumble.

"Brother Iriel approaches the glowing mechanism," Kevin says, his voice sliding into the formal cadence of his character. "I examine the runes for any similarity to the prophecies we found in the hidden library of Vos'Kareth."

His gaze is steady and expectant, grounded in trust.

"Sir Gallant kicks one of the brass gears," Brian says, grabbing his miniature. "Gently, though. I'm not making that mistake again. No more Clockwork Dragon incidents, right?" He winks at me.

A small laugh escapes me. "You nearly got the entire party killed."

"Worth it," Brian grins.

Nate clears his throat. When he speaks, it's in Seraphiel's voice, deeper than his own, resonant with controlled power.

"While they investigate, I kneel at the edge of the platform. The corruption that once flowed through me...I can sense it in this place. Was this built by the same hands that forged my cursed blade?"

The room shifts. Something inside me steadies.

"Perception check."

Nate rolls without hesitation. "Fifteen."

A deep breath. My palms rub against my sweater, and the fear passes through me. My voice, when it returns, is softer than my DM voice of old, but it still carries authority, the simple power of continuing.

"You're right, Seraphiel. As you kneel, the runes on your sword subtly glow in sequence with the markings on the floor."

My narration explains how the chamber responds to their presence; how the archaic magic recognizes them as the heroes foretold. My hands still shake, but the words flow around the tremor. When my memory of a particular rune falters, Kevin provides it. When I can't find the right words for a demonic taunt, Brian supplies a line so perfectly in character that I have to laugh. The vision builds itself between us, a bridge across the silence.

For all these years, I gave them stories. But they gave me a reason to keep telling them.

As they reach the center, my eyes drift shut momentarily. The pain medication makes my head swim, but something else flows through me now, a current older than illness, stronger than fear.

"Seekers of the fractured path," I intone, my voice transforming into something venerable and resonant, "you stand where no mortal has stood since the Sundering. The choices that broke the world were made within these walls."

My hands rise, trembling with the power of the moment. "What was scattered must be united. What was broken must be mended. But beware, some wounds were meant to fester."

Brian erupts into laughter, that distinctive cackle I heard through headphones for a decade but never witnessed in person.

"Classic." He shakes his head. "Offering us salvation with one hand and apocalypse with the other."

My fingers press against my forehead as I lean forward, trying to recall a crucial detail.

"Wait, didn't you find something in the Obsidian Archives? That scroll with the binding ritual? Three sessions ago, when you fought the Shadowmere assassins..." My mind gropes through fog.

Kevin doesn't miss a beat. He flips open a

weathered notebook. The pages are filled with his neat handwriting, color-coded by session date.

"Session two hundred thirty-nine." He turns the notebook toward me. "Brother Iriel discovered the Scroll of Nine Bindings hidden inside a false reliquary. Here's the exact wording of the incantation, and," he points, "these were the components needed."

The precision strikes me. All these years, Kevin has been documenting every word, preserving what I thought was ephemeral. My scattered thoughts, my spontaneous world-building, collected and archived.

"Thanks." The details flood back as I look at the notes, and the story regains its shape.

Around the table, they all nod. A world imagined together that feels as real as this room.

Nate leans forward, his posture looser than when he arrived. The tightness around his eyes has softened. He places both palms on the table, and when he speaks, it's with Seraphiel's measured cadence.

"I step forward," he says, meeting my gaze for the first time. "If this place holds the key to my redemption, then I will be the one to bear whatever price it demands."

Something extraordinary happens. The pain in my joints recedes. The heaviness in my lungs lightens. For a precious moment, we aren't in my office with its pill bottles and medical equipment. We're in the brass chamber beneath a city of eternal flame, facing destinies we've crafted together word by word, roll by roll.

One by one, I take them in. Not Sir Gallant, Brother Iriel, and Seraphiel. But Brian, who flew three hours after closing a sales meeting. Kevin, who rearranged his entire library schedule. Nate, who conquered debilitating anxiety to board a plane.

Ten years. Of voices through headphones, of friendship transmitted through Ethernet cables and Wi-Fi signals. We built something extraordinary in that digital space, but what could we have been to each other if we'd been brave enough to bridge this gap sooner? How many dinners could we have shared? How many conversations mattered? How many moments like this one—real faces, real laughter, real presence?

The lament cuts deep. I spent so long teaching literature students about missed connections and tragic timing, without recognizing my own story unfolding in real time. We could have discovered that pixels and voices were only the beginning, that the magic we created in Eldyrane was nothing compared to sitting around an actual table, breathing the same air.

But perhaps that's not fair to what we have. Maybe those years of careful distance were necessary, a safe space to become ourselves before we could risk being seen. Maybe we needed the armor of avatars before we could stand to be vulnerable in each other's presence.

A complete smile extends across my face. It isn't theatrical, nor is it laced with the performative thrill of epic battles. It's muted. Genuine. A warm recognition of what we've created.

They never needed a dungeon. They just needed something to keep walking through together.

Cure Light Wounds

Walt opens the door, and I catalog the moment methodically. His appearance: thirty percent less body mass than estimated from our last video call three years ago. Posture: diminished by fifteen degrees. Skin tone: sallow, with pronounced capillary visibility. His sweater hangs from shoulders that once carried the weight of entire fictional civilizations.

Unanticipated: the visceral tightening in my throat.

I nod respectfully, hoping the gesture will communicate the volumes I would like to speak.

Walt stares at us with visible shock. His hand trembles against the doorframe though he tries to hide it. Brian fidgets beside me, his nervous energy radiating like heat as Nate fixes his stare at the ground. We're strangers who know each other better than most families.

Ellen leads us inside. The house is exactly as I'd visualized it from Walt's occasional descriptions: craftsman-style bookshelves, academic diplomas, framed maps of real and imaginary places. Each detail is filed away into the mental database I've maintained for 3,642 days.

When we enter his office, I pause. Ellen has

arranged everything with unexpected precision. A card table positioned elegantly for four players. Walt's recliner at the head, with three folding chairs surrounding it. Players' places arranged with graph paper, dice, and little pencils.

Twice monthly for ten years, this game has been the singular consistent social interaction in my life that wasn't a student asking for an obscure research paper. The one place people expected me to show up. The only people who noticed when I didn't.

Nate's fingers work a stimming pattern against his thighs, and I'm transported back to six years ago. I'd been shelving returns in the psychology stacks when I spotted it: *Uniquely Human: A Different Way of Seeing Autism* by Barry Prizant. Something about the author's affirming perspective, viewing autism as a different way of being rather than something to be fixed, made me think of Nate immediately.

It wasn't the first time I'd connected a book to one of our group. Twenty-three years as a university librarian at Brown teaches you to read between the lines; of books, and people. The teenager who keeps checking out fantasy novels isn't solely escaping; she's searching for heroes to see herself in. The postgrad who requests biographies of failed entrepreneurs isn't researching success; he's processing his own disappointments.

With Nate, there were signs. His careful word choices in our chat sessions. The way he'd go silent when conversations moved too fast, then return with perfectly articulated thoughts. His Seraphiel was eloquent, controlled, everything Nate seemed to struggle to be in casual conversation.

I'd sent him the eBook with a simple note: "Thought you might find this interesting. No response needed." For two months, nothing. Then, a single private message: "Enjoyed this very much. This was thoughtful. Thank you."

Nine words that told me everything. He'd read it. He'd understood why I'd sent it. It felt good. A little like healing, a lot like Brother Iriel. I set my bag down carefully, maintaining composure on the outside while something essential threatens to crack within.

My character sheet is aligned precisely one inch from the table's edge. Mechanical pencil to the right, eraser positioned for maximum efficiency. Dice arranged by value, d20 front and center, the others in descending order. When the world tilts unpredictably, precision anchors me.

"Session two hundred forty-two," I say, flipping through my journal while Brian gawks.

Library science taught me that proper categorization isn't strictly about finding things; it's about preserving them. And I've preserved everything: every description Walt ever crafted, every plot twist, every throwaway line that made us laugh until our headsets crackled with distortion.

Walt's fingers tremble when he reaches for his dice. His breathing changes after speaking more than a few sentences. There's a slight wince when he shifts position. My eyes flick to the doorway where Ellen appears briefly, checking in, her eyes tracking Walt's water glass, the medication schedule I glimpsed stuck to the refrigerator.

Brian makes another joke about Sir Gallant's past misadventures, and Walt chuckles. The sound activates something in me, a data point that alters my projections. Walt's laugh is weaker than in my memory, but his eyes still light up with enthusiasm.

I make a notation in the margin of my notes. *Session*

242 resumed after 97-day hiatus. Ambient temperature 72°F. Participants: all present.

"Intelligence check," Walt instructs, and my hand automatically reaches for my blue d20, the one I've used for Brother Iriel since session thirty-nine. The original green one cracked after a particularly tense encounter with the Shadowmere.

"Twenty-four," I announce after adding my modifiers.

What Walt doesn't know is that I've been running statistical analyses on our campaigns for years. Average damage per encounter. Success probability curves. I've documented everything because I couldn't bear to lose any of it.

I watch Walt's posture carefully. The way he leans more heavily on his right side. The slight pause before complex descriptions, as if gathering strength. Thirty minutes into the session, Ellen silently appears with fresh water and two small pills. Walt takes them with practiced discretion, thinking none of us notices.

I notice. I always notice.

"The runes speak of a binding ritual," Walt says, his hands rising to illustrate. "Something powerful was imprisoned here, something that predates the Sundering itself."

His left hand trembles mid-gesture. A micro-fraction of pain crosses his face before he smooths it away.

My stomach tightens unexpectedly. I've built my life around observation without intervention. Categorization without judgment. Recording without emotion. The perfect librarian. The perfect cleric. The background player who keeps everything running.

And I can't help him.

I flip through my journal, eleven volumes

completed, the twelfth half-filled. Thousands of pages of meticulous notes. Maps I've redrawn for clarity. Complex relationships charted with precision. Walt's opus, preserved in my handwriting.

While Nate and Brian roll for their actions, I study my friend. The paradox of him—physically diminishing yet still containing multitudes. The entire construct of Eldyrane lives in that failing body. Civilizations and magic systems and ethical dilemmas that shaped who we became as much as any real-world experience.

He gave me this. All of this. This total experience. What have I returned?

The epiphany snaps into focus, sharp as a corrected lens: my actions all these years haven't been passive. I've been building an archive. A memory vault. When Walt describes the chamber, I'm ready with the reference to the Eastern Temples from three campaigns ago. When he falters on a name, I supply it. My notes are the foundation holding our shared story together. I started taking them out of habit, a librarian's compulsion to organize information. But somewhere along the way, it became something else. When Brian made that ridiculous seduction attempt on the gelatinous cube, I didn't note *comic relief moment*. I transcribed his exact words, the way Walt's boisterous laughter filled our headsets, how even Nate broke character to giggle. When Seraphiel delivered that first stunning monologue, I captured both the dialogue and the stunned silence that followed.

Over the years, they'd started to ask: *What did the oracle say last session? How much damage did we take in that fight? What was the name of that merchant in Silverdale?* Walt would pause, waiting for my answer. Brian would interrupt his own stories to confirm details with me. Even Nate, precise as he was with his own character, relied on my records for party history. My documentation became the foundation holding our shared story together. Our collective history. The gap between sessions made it clear: without my notes, details fade. Plot threads tangle. But with them, every callback lands. Every reference connects.

My precision is devotion. And it matters enough to get exactly right.

"Brother Iriel steps forward," I say, my voice steadier than my thoughts. "I place my hands on the central rune circle and recite the binding words we found in the Obsidian Archives."

Walt appears momentarily confused.

"From the Scroll of Nine Bindings," I supply, turning my notebook toward him. "Session two-hundred thirty-nine. The exact phrasing was: 'What was broken in blood can only be mended through sacrifice.'"

Relief washes over Walt's face, both for the reminder and for something deeper. The recognition that the world he built doesn't solely depend on his failing memory anymore. It lives in my notes. In Brian's instinctive understanding of its logic. In Nate's emotional connection to its mysteries.

"Yes," Walt says, nodding. "The Scroll of Nine Bindings. Brother Iriel, your knowledge serves you well once again."

I arrange my play space in precise formation before the next roll, a ritual I've performed thousands of times. But now it feels different—a personal comfort sure, but also part of the foundation that holds all of us together.

I've always been the stoic one. The reliable one. The punctual one with the proper materials and the correct answers. I thought that made me peripheral, a supporting character in Walt's grand narrative. I thought I was taking notes. But I was building a bridge that would carry his world forward, a bridge we're walking across together now.

ALMOST FIVE HOURS IN, AND HE HAD ONLY paused twice to take his medication. Walt's narrative stumbles. There's a crucial transition missing between the initial description and the next plot point. For a few seconds, the story dangles unfinished.

"And then the lever slowly begins to—" His hand trembles violently as he reaches for the d12, knocking it off the table entirely. The die makes a hollow sound against the hardwood.

I note the time: 4:47 p.m. Medication wearing off. Increased tremor amplitude. Concentration lapses at approximately 90-minute intervals.

"I'll get that," Brian says, diving for the fallen die. "Let me roll it for you. What are we checking for? Random encounter? Trap damage?"

He's filling space with words again. Covering the moment like he's done so many times before. I understand the impulse. Redirect. Normalize. Proceed.

Nate adjusts his posture marginally, eyes fixed on his sheet. His breathing has changed—shorter inhales, longer exhales. Stress response.

I observe Walt's hand as Brian places the die back in it. The tremor worsens. Skin tone: pale. Nail beds: slightly cyanotic.

For a moment, it's not Walt's hand I see, but my father's, struggling with a jar lid he refused to let me open. This entire scene—the restrained struggle, the stubborn pride, our helpless observation—is a routine I know by heart. For almost three years, I was the archivist of my father's decline. Morning pills arranged by dosage. Afternoon blood pressure checks. Evening confusion that came and went like tide pools. He was the strongest man I ever knew; I'm fifty-one and it still feels strange when someone calls me "Mister Jeong." Watching his fierce independence slowly become a cage taught me the hardest lesson about strength: its truest form isn't refusing help, but knowing when to accept it.

Father never asked for help. Neither does Walt. Both men, who'd spent lifetimes taking care of others, suddenly forced into dependency. Those years taught me patience I didn't know I possessed. Taught me to anticipate needs without making someone feel helpless. Taught me that sometimes, the most profound act of care is to simply bear witness to a man's fight for his own dignity, right up to the end.

I'd thought I was good at it. Thought I had time to get better.

Walt coughs, and it jolts me back to attention.

"...and do you remember," he says, "the Caverns of Vos'Kareth? When Brother Iriel attempted that mass healing spell?"

My stomach clenches. *That session.* Of all the thousands of hours, why that one?

I manage a neutral nod. "Session one hundred eighty-seven. The party was critically wounded after the ambush."

"Rolled a natural one," Brian says with a laugh, slapping the table. "Total party wipe! Sir Gallant was screaming about dying a virgin for like twenty minutes."

Brian is laughing, but I'm back in my silent house, with the sympathy cards still littering the coffee table. Father had died two days before, and the grief still sat in me like a physical weight. I'd almost cancelled, sent Walt a message saying I might not make it, not wanting to explain why.

His reply was simple: *We're here if you need us. No pressure either way.*

I showed up anyway, needing the routine, the structure.

"The spell backfired," Walt continues, his eyes crinkling at the memory. "Instead of healing, it summoned those shadow wraiths."

"Technically, it was a divine channeling mishap," I correct automatically. "Page forty-two of the *Cleric's Codex*. Failure results in the opposite effect manifesting."

They're all looking at me, amused by my precision. I laugh along, but it feels empty. That night, Walt had re-configured the campaign on the fly. Changed the mission from an aggressive assault to a quest for healing old wounds. The NPCs we encountered spoke of loss and remembrance; the final hall held no treasure, only crystallized memories of lives well-lived.

"I had to use all my spell slots to keep everyone alive after that disaster," I say, trying to maintain the light tone.

Walt shifts in his chair. "But you figured out how to cast that reveal spell. Found that hidden inscription on the cavern wall."

"Only because you practically shoved it in my face," I reply.

"I don't remember it that way." His lips curl a trace.

I had thought it was a coincidence. Thought I was just projecting my grief onto the game.

But looking at Walt now, across this table, his tired eyes holding mine, the realization lands with the force of a shockwave.

He knew.

He knew, and without a single awkward word, he had rebuilt our imaginary world into a sanctuary for my real-world pain.

"Maybe that spell landed after all," I say, the words catching in my throat.

Walt's eyes meet mine, a warm understanding that needs no words. "I've always thought so."

PRESERVATION TECHNIQUES FOR AGING materials are fundamental to my background. How to control temperature and humidity. How to prevent spine damage. How to encapsulate brittle pages.

I've spent years helping the party stay alive, but I don't know how to keep the DM from dying.

The thought sits in my chest like a stone with precise dimensions: seven-point-three centimeters of helplessness. I want to speak, to acknowledge what's happening, to tell Walt what these sessions have meant. I have the vocabulary. I've read thousands of books containing millions of words for exactly this situation. But my mouth remains closed. The words arranged in my mind would disrupt the session. They would transform this space from game to goodbye. And Walt doesn't want that. This isn't about saying goodbye. It's about staying until the end.

So, I pick up my blue d20 instead. "Brother Iriel examines the glowing mechanism."

The dust-caked door opens with a grinding sound as Sir Gallant pushes forward without checking for traps. Typical Brian behavior, rushing in. But his recklessness has saved us as often as it's endangered us. The room beyond glows with eerie blue light, casting long shadows across the face of a hobbled figure.

"As you enter," Walt says, his voice stronger now, "an elderly keeper rises from his meditation. Wizened hands clutch a gnarled staff, eyes clouded with cataracts yet somehow seeing beyond the physical realm."

The keeper is clearly an extension of Walt himself, frail but mighty, a vessel of knowledge. I watch Walt inhabit this NPC, his hands rising in a protective gesture that mirrors his character's.

"Who disturbs the Chamber of Echoes?" Walt's eerie keeper voice asks.

Brian leans forward, d20 already in hand. "Sir Gallant introduces himself with a flourish and a bow. 'Just some humble adventurers seeking ancient wisdom, good sir. Perhaps you might—' wait, I want to do a perception check while I'm talking to see if there's anything valuable on him."

Walt nods. Brian rolls. *Two.*

"As you scan his wardrobe mid-conversation, your sword arm swings wide, catching the keeper across his frail shoulder."

"What? No! That wasn't—" Brian protests.

"The old man staggers back, blood blooming across his robes." Walt's hand rises to his own shoulder, a mirror of his NPC's pain.

The voice in my head whispers it's pointless, too little, too late. But my hands move anyway.

I reach for my blue d4. "Brother Iriel steps forward and casts Cure Light Wounds on the keeper."

"Roll it," Walt says.

Three. "Plus my modifier, that's seven points of healing."

"The wound closes," Walt says, his breathing labored. "The keeper nods in gratitude."

Our eyes meet across the table. His nod mirrors his NPC's, a synchronicity between storyteller and story. No thanks necessary. Ten years of silent communication.

I glance around the table. Brian is already planning his next move, dice dancing around his fingers. Nate's focus is absolute, his character sheet annotated with precise observations. All of us locked in this moment, this world. And I understand what we're doing here. We're not just playing a game. We're maintaining the structural integrity of something precious and fragile. Each roll, each spell, each shared laugh, small threads weaving a shelter around Walt.

Brother Iriel's healing spell won't fix a shattered shoulder in the real world, and it damn sure can't cure cancer. The magic stops at the edge of our sheets. My careful notes and precise rolls can't rewrite medical charts or blood counts.

I can't save him. But I can keep playing.

Chaotic Good

The smell of death hits me the moment I step through the front door. Sterile gauze, old books and something underneath that feels final. Walt's house is exactly what I imagined during all those late-night sessions: bookshelves everywhere, a worn leather armchair, and framed maps that might be fantasy or might be places I'm too ignorant to recognize.

"Nice digs, Professor!" I say. "Very wizard's tower in the retirement community."

Kevin shoots me a look, that librarian stare that can silence a room. Nate flinches.

Jesus, I talk too much.

I fuss with the shoebox of miniatures under my arm as we walk in, now self-conscious about bringing them. What was I thinking? That we'd show up and Walt would leap off his deathbed for one last epic battle? That we'd pull out the dice and everything would be like it was?

"You have a lovely home," Kevin slides his messenger bag to the side.

"It's an honor to be here, sir," Nate says to the floor.

And here I am, standing like an idiot, unable to find words that aren't jokes. In game chat, I'm first with a quip, first with a plan. On the tabletop, Sir Gallant Daggerheart never hesitates. But here, in this living room that smells like a hospital ward, I'm just Brian McKinnon, regional sales manager for Middleton Industrial, a divorced guy who still has band posters on his apartment walls at forty-eight.

I catch Ellen looking at me, evaluating. I wonder what Walt has told her about us. About me. Does she know Sir Gallant Daggerheart, the swashbuckling hero who once seduced a block of gelatin? Or does she see through to Brian, the guy whose ex-wife told him he was "exhausting" before she moved in with her sister?

I can't look at him directly. Can't process how small he seems.

"I brought snacks," I blurt, though I didn't. "Left them in the car. I'll go—"

"Brian," Walt says. My name in his mouth stops me cold.

When our eyes meet, there is recognition. A tingle starts at the base of my neck.

"I'm glad you came." His voice is warm; his smile, even more so.

My throat closes up. There's no script for this. No charisma roll that will save me. For twenty-nine years, I've been selling products nobody understands to people who don't want them, but now, when it matters, words fail me completely.

"Wouldn't miss it," I manage, my voice cracking like I'm fourteen again.

Ellen leads us to Walt's office, and I keep talking, about the trip, about Ohio weather, about nothing, filling silence with noise because silence means thinking, and thinking means feeling, and feeling means acknowledging that this is the end of something I'm not ready to lose.

I glance around the office and it is absolutely game-ready. Character sheets. Dice. The whole ritual waiting for us.

"Check out this sweet setup," I say, my voice booming. "Beats my kitchen table with the wobbly leg. I always pictured Kevin being shorter, by the way. No offense, man."

Nobody laughs. Kevin gives me another librarian stare that could curdle milk. Nate's eyes dart up from his dice for a split second before retreating to safety. The silence that follows is heavy, thick with the smell of medicine and old paper.

And in that silence, I hear her. Sarah's voice, clear as the day she packed her bags. *It's exhausting, Brian, like you're performing all the time.*

My face flushes hot. My hands feel huge and useless. I drum my fingers on my knee, a frantic rhythm to ward off the ghost in the room. I'm doing it again. Being *too much*. My one-man variety show, playing to an empty house. I've spent ten years with these guys, and I still don't know what to do with my hands.

I look at Walt, who is lowering himself into his recliner. He tries to hide a wince, but I see it. The sight of his pain is a life raft. Something real to focus on.

I grab onto a memory, a real one this time, one where my jokes actually worked.

"Hey," I say, a little too loudly, desperate to change the channel. "Remember when Sir Gallant tried to seduce that dragon? And I rolled a natural one and..."

"Set the whole tavern on fire," Walt finishes, his eyes crinkling.

A genuine smile. Not pity. Relief washes over me so

fast I feel lightheaded. Okay. Good. We're on familiar ground now. I'm not just Brian, the divorced sales guy in a Journey t-shirt. Here, I can be someone else. Someone better.

Kevin's mouth twitches, the closest thing to a smile I've seen from him yet. "Forty-seven damage. I used every healing spell I had."

"Worth it," I say, and this time, the laughter feels real. But then I look at Walt, really take him in, and the back of my neck prickles. His hands tremble as he reaches for his notes. This isn't a tavern fire Sir Gallant can joke his way out of.

Kevin sits like he's at a job interview, back straight, portfolio placed precisely at the table's edge. His real-life voice matches his online one: measured, and a little stuffy. Only now I can see how his eyes flicker with concentration when he speaks, gathering information like he's filing it away in that librarian brain of his.

And Nate. Jesus. In the game, Seraphiel delivers these epic monologues that leave us all speechless, but the real Nate barely makes eye contact, his long fingers constantly adjusting and readjusting his dice like they're tiny spacecraft that need perfect alignment. When he talks, his voice comes out so soft it sounds like the speaker is broken.

But then Walt speaks, and the world shifts.

"The brass gears turn with agonizing slowness," he says, his voice fuller, transformed into the commanding presence I've heard through my headset for a decade. "Revealing a chamber that hasn't seen light in thousands of years."

Gone is the frail man in the recliner. In his place sits the Dungeon Master, who once narrated the fall of empires and the rise of heroes.

"Wait," Kevin says, reaching into his messenger bag. "Let me get my notes."

He pulls out a leather-bound journal, its edges worn from use. The pages are color-coded, tabbed, and organized with a librarian's precision. Of course Kevin has notes. Meticulous, comprehensive, marvelous notes.

I feel a familiar pang of uselessness. A tech genius, a college librarian... and me, the lubricants guy.

"Session two hundred forty-two," Kevin says, flipping through pages covered in neat handwriting. "After we defeated the Shadowmere assassins... Walt described it as 'an intricate lattice of brass and silver...'"

Walt is narrating the creation of a world. I spend my days stifling giggles during product demonstrations of *Maximum Thrust Bearing Grease*. The thought almost makes me laugh. Almost. That old dream of my band opening for Pearl Jam feels pathetic in this room, a faded story next to the vibrant one unfolding on this table.

I lean over to look at Kevin's notes, genuinely impressed. "We should pitch in and get you a stenography machine." My voice sounds too loud again.

Nate peers at the notebook too, a hint of a smile tugging at his lips. "I remember that. Seraphiel investigated the runes while Brother Iriel cataloged them."

"And Sir Gallant got bored and started pressing random buttons," Walt adds, his eyes crinkling.

We all laugh and the tension in the room dissolves like a gummy bear in Coke, and for a second, I forget about the job I'm too scared to leave. Here at least my chaos has a purpose.

I straighten my shoulders and clear my throat. When I speak, it's in Sir Gallant's cocky drawl—the voice I've used a thousand times but never in front of actual humans.

"Well, gentlemen," I declare, picking up my mini, "while you scholarly types waste time with your books and runes, Sir Gallant Daggerheart believes in the timeless tradition of pushing shiny things just to find out what happens."

My voice wobbles at first, self-consciousness creeping in, but then I notice Walt's smile widen, and something clicks into place. I settle deeper into the character, the way I do when I sit in the glow of my computer screen.

"I approach the largest gear and give it a solid poke with my dagger. After all," I add with Gallant's signature smirk, "size matters when you're handling dangerous equipment."

Kevin groans. Nate makes a choked sound that might be laughter. Walt's eyes dance with amusement.

"Roll a Dexterity check," Walt says, and the familiar command sends a shiver down my spine.

I grab my die, the lucky red one with gold flecks that's seen me through every campaign, and let it tumble across the table.

"Natural seventeen," I say, adding with Gallant's swagger, "plus my dexterity modifier of five, that's twenty-two total. Sir Gallant may be reckless, but his hands are as skilled as they are beautiful."

"As your dagger touches the gear," Walt continues, his voice gaining strength with each word, "the entire structure shudders. The brass teeth interlock with the silver components, and a low hum vibrates through the floor."

Walt's hand starts to shake badly, but before I can

do anything, the dice and his wedding ring go skittering across the table. He looks down, his cheeks flushing red. I reach over, pick up his ring and place it down softly next to him; no one-liners here, just a small gesture of respect for someone who deserves so much more.

Kevin leans forward, bringing us back into the game. "Brother Iriel examines the runes for any similarity to the prophecies we found in the hidden library of Vos'Kareth. "

"Intelligence check," Walt says.

Kevin rolls, adding numbers in his head faster than I can blink. "Twenty-four."

"The runes speak of a binding ritual," Walt says, his hands rising to illustrate his words. "Something powerful was imprisoned here. Something that predates the Sundering itself."

Nate, who has been keeping to himself, sits straighter. When he speaks, his voice drops an octave into Seraphiel's solemn baritone. "I place my hand on my cursed blade. Does it react to the energy in this place?"

As easy as that, we're back. All the awkwardness, the months of separation, the looming grief—it doesn't disappear, but it steps back, giving space for something else. Something bright and alive and ours.

I'm not Brian the loser anymore. I'm Sir Gallant Daggerheart, rogue extraordinaire, wielder of daggers and terrible pickup lines. And for once, my endless stream of jokes isn't annoying or exhausting; it's part of the tapestry we're weaving together.

Walt's eyes meet mine across the table, and I like to think I see a hint of appreciation for what I bring to this circle. The laughter. The moments of unexpected brilliance between the bad puns.

I have never felt more useful in my life.

Walt's voice grows stronger with each passing minute, his frail body feeding off the energy in the room as he weaves our story back to life. I'm settled into Sir Gallant's skin now, the character flowing through me as naturally as breathing. It's weird, all the years of playing together, and I've never seen these guys in person until today. But I know them. I honestly know them.

"As you approach the central platform," Walt continues, "tendrils of arcane energy pulse along the floor."

Kevin studies his notes with librarian precision. "I am searching for any connection to the runes we found in the eastern temples."

Nate mumbles something about sensing dark energy, his physical awkwardness vanishing when Seraphiel speaks.

And me? I'm doing what Sir Gallant does best: being impulsive.

"I'm going to check if there's anything worth pocketing in here," I say, rattling my dice. "Old brass room's gotta have some valuables, right?"

"Roll investigation," Walt chuckles, a sound so warm and familiar it's hard to believe I'm hearing it in person for the first time.

The die tumbles across the table. "Fourteen—plus five—nineteen."

Walt leans forward in his recliner, his eyes twinkling. "You find a small alcove containing crystalline objects. They pulse with inner flame— valuable, certainly, but dangerous to touch."

"Danger's my middle name," I say with Sir Gallant's swagger.

"Actually," Walt says casually, "I believe your

middle name is 'Bad Idea,' after that time you tried to pickpocket a fire elemental and ended up with third-degree burns on both hands."

I freeze, my dice halfway to my palm.

That was six years ago. A throwaway moment in a side quest. I made a stupid decision, rolled terribly, and spent the next three sessions with my character's hands bandaged, unable to use his daggers. I bring it up sometimes as one of Sir Gallant's legendary screw-ups, but I always thought I was the only one who remembered it.

But Walt does. In detail.

"You... you remember that?" The words come out strained.

Walt tilts his head, confused by my reaction. "Of course. The Temple of Eternal Flame. Sir Gallant declared, and I quote, 'How hot could it really be?' right before attempting to lift the elemental's coin purse."

Something cracks inside me. A hairline fracture in the wall I've built to keep the real world separate from this one.

He remembered my stupid joke.

All these years, I thought I was background noise between Kevin's strategy and Nate's dramatic monologues. The comic relief who kept things from getting too serious.

But Walt was listening. Really listening.

My father never listened like that. Hell, Dad never listened at all. "Going to get milk," he'd said when I was twelve, and apparently the corner store was in Brazil because we never saw him again. Mom pretended it was temporary for about three months before she stopped setting a place for him at dinner. I spent years wondering what I'd done wrong. Was I too loud? Too needy? Too fat? Maybe if I'd been funnier, smarter, thinner; maybe he would have stayed. Maybe he would have wanted to stick around and see who I became.

Walt stuck around. For ten years, he showed up every other Saturday, rain or shine, good mood or bad. He laughed at my jokes, not the polite laugh you give someone you're trying to humor, but the authentic kind—from the belly. He remembered my stories. He made space for my stupidity and somehow turned it into something valuable.

My eyes settle on this dying man, offering us the last of his energy, and I realize he has been a kind of father to me. He never gave speeches or handed down life lessons, but he showed up. He saw me. And he chose, time and again, to keep me around.

"Yeah," I manage, clearing the sudden thickness from my throat. "Gallant's not exactly known for his risk assessment skills."

Kevin smirks. "That's putting it mildly."

But I barely hear him. I'm watching Walt, whose eyes hold a knowing warmth that cuts straight through my defenses.

I reach for my dice, my fingers clumsy. I've been treating this like a favor, showing up for a dying man's last hurrah. But it isn't a favor. It's a gift, and it works both ways.

"Well," I say, straightening in my chair, "Sir Gallant has learned his lesson about fire. Mostly." I pause, then add with genuine feeling, "But he never backs down from an adventure."

Walt's smile widens, and I make a silent promise to myself. This session isn't going to be half-assed. No checking my phone under the table. No drifting off when it isn't my turn. I'm going to give everything I have to this game. Pour every ounce of creativity and enthusiasm into Sir Gallant.

Because Walt deserves it. Because he's been giving us his best for years while I thought no one was paying attention.

I lean forward, fully present in a way I haven't been in years, maybe my whole life. "So, about these fiery crystals? Any chance they'd make excellent throwing weapons if I wrapped them in cloth first?"

Saving Throw

Airports contain exactly thirty-four specific sounds that hurt. I've counted them. The high whine of the Rolls-Royce jet engines. Luggage wheels with one bad bearing. Children's voices at frequencies that penetrate bone. The waiting area alone is responsible for twenty-one of them. Gate announcements through malfunctioning speakers. Incessant beeping and chirping of various machines. Travelers arguing with airline staff at unnecessary volume levels.

My hands keep their steady rhythm against my thighs: one-two-three, one-two-three, as I try to focus on the design of the carpet beneath my feet. Blue-gray hexagons with red triangles. Repeating. Predictable. Safe.

The message from Ellen sits in my phone like a fuse: *Walt doesn't have much time left. The other guys are coming. I know it's a lot to ask but, he'd love to see you, Nate.*

I haven't been on a plane before. Ever. Too small. Too many people. No exit route.

But it's Walt.

So I booked the ticket. Picked up the anxiety medication. Wrote out every step of the journey on index cards.

The call for boarding incites the frenzy. One hundred twenty-four passengers funnel through a single doorway. Bodies in uncomfortable proximity. The man behind me breathes through his mouth. The woman ahead smells of burned coffee. I count steps to maintain focus: forty-six from gate to aircraft door.

Statistical probability suggested that the middle seat in my row would remain empty, but a large man in a Seahawks t-shirt settles beside me, claiming both armrests. His elbow touches mine. I remove my arm, place it in my lap and shift toward the window. Counting rivets in the wing housing provides temporary respite: two hundred thirteen visible from this angle.

Turbulence begins over Colorado. Logical mind knows it's air pressure differentials. Wind shear. Completely normal atmospheric phenomena. But nervous system interprets each jolt as imminent catastrophe. Hands pick up the rhythm again: one-two-three, one-two-three.

I do it for Walt.

Walt, who never rushed me when I needed three minutes and forty-two seconds of silence before responding to an NPC. Walt, who incorporated my fifteen-page multi-generational backstory into the campaign without changing a single detail. Walt, who once said, "Seraphiel's monologues are the backbone of this story."

There's safety in order. In turns. In knowing when it's your move.

That's what Seraphiel would say. That's what I told myself as the plane landed and my stomach tumbled in geometric swirls of dread.

Brian sees me before I see him; my height and awkward gait are apparently enough to identify me.

His voice is louder in person, bouncing off the terminal walls as he waves.

"Nate! Holy shit, you're a giant! I thought Kevin would be the tall one!"

He's a heavyset man with thinning hair, and he holds a sign with a single word: SERAPHIEL.

Not Nathan Abelman. Not Nate.

Seraphiel.

My body tenses, hands clenching and unclenching at my sides. Seventeen people turn to look.

Brian's voice matches the one from my headphones, but seeing the words come from an actual mouth, watching his hands gesture as he talks, creates a weird lag, like I'm watching a dubbed movie.

"H-hello," I manage, eyes fixed on the sign rather than his face.

Kevin stands beside him, just as I'd imagined. Tall, precise, a leather messenger bag hanging from one shoulder. He doesn't attempt a handshake, just nods. "Good flight?"

I manage a nod back. Words are stuck somewhere between brain and mouth. This happens. Body refusing to cooperate with my mind. In my head, I'm eloquent. Out here, I'm static.

"Ellen's waiting with the car," Brian continues, filling the silence I've created. "She's great, man. Made cookies. Homemade for the drive."

The cookies most likely have nuts. I don't eat nuts. But I don't say this.

Ellen gives me the front passenger seat. I'm tallest, she says, but I know it's because she noticed my hands fluttering when Brian suggested we all squeeze in the back. I'm thankful.

"Walt's been talking about you boys for days," she says as we drive. Her voice is gentle, like Ydrin, the librarian at the College of Liraethal. "Especially you, Nate. He says your paladin is the moral center of the campaign."

My face burns. Pride and grief tangle together in my stomach.

"Seraphiel's not moral," I say, the words coming out abruptly. Too harsh. I try again. "He's seeking redemption. It's...different."

Ellen smiles. "That sounds like something Walt would say."

The world outside the car window moves too quickly. Trees and houses and people blend into a ribbon of information my brain struggles to process. But inside the car, there's order. Kevin has his notebook open, reviewing notes. Brian talks, a steady stream that requires no response from me. Ellen drives with both hands on the wheel, exactly at the speed limit. They're not trying to fix me. Or change me. They're letting me...be.

WALT'S HOUSE IS YELLOW WITH WHITE TRIM. A garden with twenty-six distinct colors and no discernible pattern. Concrete steps leading to a front door with a weathered mat that says, "Adventure Awaits."

I stare at it while Ellen rings the doorbell. My pulse quickens so much I can feel my shirt vibrating.

This is wrong. Walt is supposed to be a storyteller, a presence, a creator. Not a person in a house with a doormat and cancer. Not someone who's dying.

"You okay?" Kevin asks.

I'm not. But I made it this far.

The door opens. The smell hits me first: a library, if it existed in the middle of a hospital. Then Walt himself, standing in the hallway, bracing himself against the wall.

He's so much smaller than his voice. Frailer than the kingdoms he's ruled. His hands shake as he greets us, and something twists inside me.

I manage to hold his gaze for two-point-seven seconds before looking away. Longer than I can usually manage with strangers. But Walt isn't a stranger. Walt knows me better than anyone in my real life, even though this is the first time I've looked into his eyes.

"Nate," he says, and his voice is the same as in our sessions, but weaker. "You came all this way."

I nod, words stuck behind the pressure in my throat. I want to tell him that Seraphiel would cross oceans for his oath-brother. That I would cross something even more terrifying, like the sky itself, for him.

But all I can manage is, "Yes, sir."

The ceiling fan in the living room rotates at approximately seventy-two RPM. I count to keep myself centered as he walks us down the hallway. Walt's office feels like a sanctuary. Books everywhere, the kind of organized disorder that makes sense to me. Ellen has set up a card table with three folding chairs arranged around Walt's recliner, which acts as our makeshift gaming table. I take the chair closest to the window. Brian settles across from me, still fidgeting with his d20. Kevin arranges his materials with the same precision I do; always imagined he did, nice to know for sure. For the first time since I left home this morning, I feel my shoulders relax slightly.

This is what I came for. Not the awkward small talk and eye contact, but sitting around a table with people who understand me. Where I can be a part of something rather than apart from things.

Walt watches us get settled and, despite his frailty, there's something in his eyes that makes this all worthwhile. The same light that's guided us through ten years of adventures.

"So," he says, voice gaining strength. "Ready to find out what happens next?"

For the first time all day, the answer is simple.

THE HEFT OF THE D20 IN MY HAND FEELS different here. Familiar but strange. Like finding your toothbrush in someone else's bathroom. My fingers trace the edges: twenty sides, each one a possible fate. The opalescent shimmer catches the light from Walt's desk lamp at different angles. Too many to count, though I try.

I adjust my belt. Brown leather with a simple silver buckle. Not special to anyone else, but I bought it the day after I created Seraphiel. When I wear it, my posture improves. My voice steadies. It's a mask that doesn't seem so suffocating.

I put it on this morning before going to the airport. The pull of it around my waist grounds me. Things don't seem as slippery.

"Seraphiel approaches the central mechanism," I say, and the voice that emerges isn't mine. It's deeper. Steadier. It flows from somewhere beneath my constantly knotted stomach, past the places where words usually tangle.

The tremor that usually lives in my hands disappears when I speak as him. The belt helps anchor me. It always has.

Walt nods, his eyes brightening despite the pallor beneath. "The mechanism responds to your presence,

Seraphiel. The runes on your blade pulse in rhythm with the markings etched into the floor."

My spine straightens. In this moment, the office walls fade away. The crushing awareness of my body in an unfamiliar space; too tall, too awkward, too much, dissolves. I'm no longer Nathan Abelman, IT technician who needed three Xanax to board a plane. I'm Seraphiel the Broken, an Oathbreaker seeking redemption.

"I place my palm against the largest gear," I continue, my voice resonating at a frequency that feels impossible outside this circle. "If this aged magic recognizes the corruption in my blood, then perhaps it also holds the key to cleansing it."

Brian grins, leaning forward. "Sir Gallant stands ready, daggers drawn. You know, just in case your dark magic stuff goes sideways. Again."

Kevin adjusts his glasses. "Brother Iriel transcribes the runes, seeking patterns from the ancient texts."

They don't flinch. Don't shift uncomfortably. Don't exchange glances that say *Here he goes again*. They simply… respond. Like my words belong in the space between us. No one mentions my knee bouncing or the tapping on my thighs. No one suggests I should make more eye contact or speak louder. Kevin doesn't slow down his speech or use simple words. Brian doesn't explain social cues I've missed. They've never asked what's "wrong" with me or offered unsolicited handshakes.

For ten years, they've treated Seraphiel, and by extension, me, as an equal member of the party. My tactical suggestions carry the same weight as Kevin's research or Brian's creative mayhem. When I deliver a monologue, they listen with genuine attention, not patronizing patience.

They value what I create. Seraphiel's moral complexity. His struggle for redemption. The philosophical questions I weave into his choices. Not once has anyone suggested I should play a simpler character or tone down the elaborate backstory. Around this table, I'm not the odd one out. We all are, and somehow that makes us fit together perfectly.

WE BROKE FOR LUNCH AFTER A FEW HOURS. IT was hushed, and awkward: microwaved cream of mushroom soup and turkey sandwiches on mismatched plates. Brian told a long, meandering story about a client who tried to pay him in cryptocurrency. Kevin took notes while pretending not to. I counted the number of bites it took Walt to finish half a sandwich: twenty-three. Then he pushed the plate away.

The afternoon light shifted in the room. Shadow angles lengthened, the ceiling fan ticking louder as the temperature dropped slightly. When Walt proposed, "Shall we return?" it felt like the most logical thing in the world.

The words flow effortlessly when I'm Seraphiel. In Eldyrane, I understand the rules. I know the right thing to say and when to say it. The sheets are organized. The story has structure. The time passes unnoticed.

The party ventures further inward, and Walt tells us in pinpoint detail how it reacts to our presence. "The runes on Seraphiel's blade glow with increasing intensity. A voice, wizened and resonant, speaks directly into your mind: 'The price of redemption is memory, Seraphiel. What would you sacrifice to be whole again?'"

I close my eyes, feeling Seraphiel settle around me like a second skin. The words rise effortlessly.

"I raise my blade before me, its corrupted edge catching the ethereal light," I say, my hands mimicking the gesture without conscious thought. "I would sacrifice everything but my oath to protect these companions. They are the only pure thing I have known in this broken existence."

Brian whistles low. Kevin nods approvingly. Walt's eyes meet mine, a direct gaze I can hold only in this sacred space between real and imagined.

"The voice appears pleased with your answer," Walt says, a smile softening his tired face. "The corruption in your blade dims — unchanged in form, yet no longer ignored. Understood. Accepted."

I feel warmth in the middle of my body, radiating outward.

I think it's happiness.

Not the cautious contentment of a neatly ordered workspace or when my code compiles on the first try. This is something wilder, less contained. Something that exists only in the intersection between game and reality; where I am both myself and not-myself. Where my words flow unobstructed by the tangles in my brain.

Seraphiel would die for these men. So I can be brave through him.

And for now, in this room with these people, that's enough.

"There is an energy here, Seraphiel, do you feel it?" Walt asks.

I lean forward and something shifts inside me. "Yes, I can," I say, Seraphiel's voice carrying the toll of this campaign. "The final test approaches. Everything we've worked toward. Every choice. Every sacrifice. It all leads here."

"Each party member roll a Constitution check. This is about endurance; can your spirits withstand purification?"

We each grab our d20s and roll: sixteen; thirteen; mine tumbles across the table: eighteen.

Walt nods slowly. "You lock hands with your party. The three of you frozen in place."

Instinctively, Brian reaches his hands out for Kevin and me. I clasp his hand in mine.

Walt places his hands on the arms of his recliner and pushes himself upwards. Kevin reaches out for him, but Walt shakes his head and raises his arms. The voice that emerges is legendary.

"Brilliant light erupts from the center of the platform, washing over Seraphiel in waves. It is cleansing. Your body shivers as the darkness is drawn directly from your soul, years of corruption stretching away like shadows at dawn."

I close my eyes, enveloped in the moment.

"Power courses through you, cascading into your party. Your limbs go cold, yet you do not fear, as a searing pain tears through your chest. The three of you fall to your knees as Seraphiel screams out in the purest agony you've ever heard."

Walt goes silent. I peek through my right eye to watch him take a deep breath.

"Both the pain and the light fade," Walt continues. "You have endured the cleansing."

"That wasn't so bad, huh?" Brian quips.

Across the table, Kevin is furiously writing in his notebook.

"You open your eyes, and before you lies a leather satchel, simple but beautifully crafted."

"I pick it up," I say immediately. "What is it?"

Walt's voice shakes with timeless authority. "It is the living record of your journey, written in the blood of those you've lost, preserved in the tears of those you've saved. Your redemption, Seraphiel, is complete and eternal." He turns his gaze directly upon me. "You have no memory of what has occurred."

Walt's smile is radiant.

The room vibrates with his words as he spreads his arms wide. "The chamber shakes with divine power, beginning to rise, carrying you back toward the City of Brass and—"

His voice cuts off abruptly. A strange, wet sound replaces his words.

I don't move. Can't move. My fingers freeze on my die, halfway through my habitual rotation.

Walt coughs. Not the polite kind. This is violent, deep, wrong. His body convulses forward over the table, his hand clutching at his chest.

"Walt?" Brian stands, knocking his chair back three inches. "Walt, you okay?"

Kevin leans forward, reaching across. "Walt, do you need water?"

I remain still. This wasn't in the campaign notes. There was no foreshadowing for this encounter.

My mind races through rulebooks and player guides. What save does Walt need to roll? Constitution? Fortitude? What's the DC threshold? Is this a status effect or direct damage?

But the numbers won't come. The systems fail me.

"Ellen!" Kevin calls sharply, his voice pitched thirty-three percent higher than his normal speaking tone. "Ellen, we need you!"

Brian's hand hovers near Walt's shoulder, uncertain. "Should I? Do we?"

Walt coughs again, a crimson spray speckling the table. One droplet lands on my character sheet, directly on the 'h' in Seraphiel. It leeches into the parchment-colored paper, the ink warping around it.

Kevin stands, phone already in hand. "I'm calling nine-one-one."

Ellen appears in the doorway, moving faster than seems possible for her age.

Something is breaking inside me. The careful order I've maintained, the separation between Seraphiel's world and mine, collapses like poorly stacked dice. In the game, death has rules. Hit points. Saving throws. But Walt is dying by different ones now. Rules I never learned how to navigate.

My hands begin their self-soothing: one-two-three, one-two-three, as Ellen cradles Walt's head against her, murmuring words I cannot process.

She's rocking softly, her hand moving through his hair, sobbing as she dabs the blood from his mouth. The sound has weight, mass, density. I can feel it pressing against my skin.

Then Walt's coughing stops. His body is still.

The blood droplet on my sheet is drying to rust-brown, an imperfect circle with fractal edges.

It's been less than a minute. I need to hurry.

My hands move without conscious direction, reaching into my dice bag. A special pouch—separate, sealed. Special dice I've never rolled before. Reserved for one purpose.

"Nate," Kevin says. His voice registers at exactly forty-two decibels. Lower than normal speaking volume.

I don't respond. The Player's Handbook is clear on this. Page 272: "Revivify requires diamonds worth at least 300 gold pieces, which the spell consumes."

I've prepared for this. From my pocket, I withdraw a small vial. Inside, dust from a diamond cutting machine at my work, collected meticulously over months, stored away for emergencies. Light catches the particles, sparkling rainbows.

"Material," I explain, voice flat. Function over form.

Brian stands behind Ellen, his hands on her shoulders, eyes wet. Kevin remains still, watching me without interfering.

I move to Walt's side, uncork the vial, and pour the diamond dust in a circle around his wrist. His skin is cooling, approximately two-point-seven degrees below normal body temperature.

"The spell requires verbal, somatic, and material components," I state, because rules must be followed precisely.

Nobody contradicts me. That means they understand. They see what I see.

I place my palm against Walt's arm, feel the absence of pulse. I begin the incantation not in Nate's stuttering words but Seraphiel's confident ones. The paladin's voice flows through me, deep and resonant.

"By ancient power and oaths unbroken; return to us in state awoken; heal and restore, awake and survive; bring back to life, this body revive!"

My hand doesn't shake as I lift the black and golden die. Twenty sides of possibility. Probability. The universe distilled to numbers and chance.

"DC fifteen for revivify under Eldyrane rules," I explain. "Plus four for target age. Minus two for caster level. Final DC seventeen."

I roll.

The die tumbles across the card table in a looping path, physics and momentum playing their parts. It settles.

Nineteen.

A success. Two points above the required threshold.

I wait. The rules are absolute. The universe must comply.

One second passes. Two. Three.

Walt remains still. Ellen's rocking continues.

I glance at the die again. *Nineteen* stares back at me.

"It should have worked," I say, my voice rough. My fingers tap against my thigh: one-two-three, one-two-three. "I followed the rules. I used the components. I passed the check."

Kevin stands next to me and I look at him. "It should have worked."

No response. Just his hand on my shoulder, steady pressure.

The game has rules. Life should have rules too. That's the promise.

Brian kneels beside me, arm around my back. Kevin remains on my other side. Neither speaks. Neither explains the contradiction between my successful roll and Walt's continued stillness. Ellen sobs.

They're here with me in the silence, in the space between worlds where dice can't save us, where the most important spell on my list means nothing against reality's cruel randomness.

I close my fingers around the die. *Nineteen.* A success that failed.

At once, the rules I've trusted all my life make no sense at all.

Above Table

I knew their voices long before I knew their faces. For ten years, they visited my home every other Saturday, laughter erupting through walls, battles raging in the distance as I did the dishes. Solemn moments of storytelling that made me pause with dishtowel in hand.

The laundry room shared a wall with Walt's office. I'd fold clothes during their sessions, smiling at the battles and bickering, the triumphs and failures. Sometimes I'd bring Walt tea just to glimpse the transformation, to witness the private professor recede and a grand storyteller take his place, his voice a chorus of a dozen different men and monsters, hands spinning yarns in the air. Walt's glow in those moments—that was the man I married. He was the builder of worlds, the man behind the mild professor who spoke softly at faculty dinners.

"Ellen, you should join sometime," Walt would say after sessions ended.

I always declined. "It's your sacred space," I'd tell him. And it was. In that room, with those men, my gentle, soft-spoken husband transformed. He became emperors and dragons, gods and villains. He architected worlds with words that even I, who shared his bed for forty-three years, had never heard him speak aloud.

Our Sunday breakfast became my window into Eldyrane. Walt would sit forward, eyes bright, explaining plot threads and character arcs over pancakes. "Nate's paladin is wrestling with redemption," he'd say, or "Sir Gallant nearly destroyed an entire city last night with one bad roll." I'd nod, not understanding the mechanics but the joy they brought him.

I remember how the oncologist's words hung in the air like smoke: "Pancreatic adenocarcinoma. Stage four. I'm very sorry, Mr. Lennox." Walt went still beside me, his hand tightening around mine. I heard myself asking practical questions about treatment options, timelines, and what to expect, while something cold and fractured spread through my body.

On the drive home, we barely spoke. Walt stared out the passenger window, and I focused on the road, the familiar route we'd driven thousands of times. When we pulled into our driveway, neither of us moved to get out. We sat there in the car as if we were afraid the house might be different now. That everything would be different now.

"I should call the university," he said. "Arrange for someone to cover my classes."

"Not yet," I offered. "Let's just... sit with this for a while."

That night, he went to his office and closed the door. I heard him moving around, organizing papers, closing binders. When he came to bed, he was somber. The next morning, he was withdrawn. Soon, the sessions slowed, then stopped. His friends drifted, not from lack of caring, but because Walt wouldn't reach out. Wouldn't let them see him diminished. I watched my husband fade—first from illness, then from isolation. The light that carried him through all those years grew dim.

That was when I knew I had to fight for him. Walt had given up, but I hadn't. So I did what he never would. I called them. Invited them. Set the stage for one last session.

"They won't come," Walt had said when I first floated the idea. "They have lives, Ellen."

But I knew better. I'd seen the concern in their emails, understood the subtext in the casual messages asking for updates. These men, who had never met in person, shared something deeper than friendship.

If Walt wouldn't sanction it, then I would undertake my own secret quest: to unite the party once again. Kevin accepted immediately, asking if there was anything else he could do to help. Brian had a sales meeting but would make it regardless. And Nate, who was silent until one day I received an email with a date, a flight number, and the question: "Will I need to rent a car?"

On the drive to the airport that morning, I'd felt as nervous as I had on my wedding day. Would they recognize me from Walt's descriptions? Would they understand why I'd orchestrated this reunion in secret?

The arrivals board showed Brian's flight from Cincinnati had landed twenty minutes early. I stood near baggage claim with a handwritten sign reading "McKinnon," feeling foolish and exposed. What if this entire plan was a mistake?

But when a burly man with thinning hair spotted my sign and broke into a huge grin, I knew immediately it wasn't. The energy was unmistakably Brian, as Walt had always characterized him.

"You must be Ellen!" His voice filled the terminal. "Holy shit—sorry, holy cow—you're exactly how Walt described you." Kevin walked beside him, taller and more composed, extending a precise handshake.

"Thank you for arranging this," Kevin said. "Walt doesn't know we're coming?"

"Not a clue," I confirmed, leading them toward the parking garage. "Nate's flight arrives in thirty minutes."

I offered them some cookies I'd baked the night before—peanut butter chocolate-chip. Kevin politely declined, but Brian grabbed three and then stuffed another into his mouth. He turned my sign over, wrote SERAPHIEL on it, and headed back in.

When they came back with Nate, pale and anxious with his silver luggage, I watched the three of them together for the first time. The dynamic was perfect: Brian's energy, Kevin's stability, and Nate's intensity. Walt's chosen family, complete. I'd expected them to be awkward strangers, but they fell into an easy rhythm—the same partnership Walt had described from their campaigns. As we drove on the interstate, I realized I wasn't taking these men to say goodbye—I was escorting them to continue the story. I couldn't give Walt more time. But I could give him the ending he wanted, surrounded by the companions that made him feel most alive, most himself.

Settling into the worn leather armchair in the living room, I pretended to read but really just listened to the symphony coming from Walt's office. The door was cracked open enough that I could hear everything without intruding. Brian's booming laugh punctuated Kevin's measured responses, while Nate's voice emerged only in character, transformed from whispers to declarations. And Walt... my Walt's voice soared above them all, stronger than it had been in months.

For hours, I listened to explorers adventure and friends reminisce. The laughter that flowed from that room washed over me like medicine—real medicine, not the amber bottles lining our countertops. Not the chemicals I'd been faithfully administering every two hours, charting side effects in my little notebook. None of those pills could produce what I heard now: Walt, fully alive again.

After a quick break for lunch, they were back at it again. From out here, I'd never have known that these men, these companions, hadn't spent a single moment in the same room. After all those years of eavesdropping through the wall, this was like finally seeing your favorite artist live after only having heard the records.

I was rinsing coffee mugs when Kevin's voice cut through the house.

"Ellen!" Panic edged his normally measured tone. "We need you!"

I knew instantly.

I dropped the mug in the sink and ran, my arthritic knees carrying me faster than they had in decades. Adrenaline is a cruel magic that way—it gives you speed when you least want to arrive.

Walt was hunched over the table. Blood at the corners of his mouth. I pushed past Brian's frozen form and gathered Walt into my arms, cradling him against my chest as I had done through every treatment, every long night.

"Walt," I whispered, rocking him gently. "I'm here. Stay with us, love."

His eyes found mine, still the same brilliant blue

that had caught my attention forty-five years ago. His lips moved, struggling to form words as his breath rattled between coughs.

"Thank you," he managed, the words barely audible.

Then, he was gone. Just like that.

Poor Nate, bless his heart, he tried. I watched through tears as he sprinkled something shimmering around Walt's wrist, rolling dice and whispering incantations like prayers.

THE PARAMEDICS ARRIVED IN A FLURRY OF efficiency and practiced calm. They spoke in a language of medical shorthand that sounded like one of Walt's invented dialects—clear to them, foreign to me. I stepped back as they surrounded him, their movements as precise as game mechanics.

"Ma'am, can you tell us what happened?" one asked, while her partner checked for vital signs we all knew weren't there.

My voice curled in my throat, thin as paper, ready to tear, so I deferred to Kevin, who answered their questions with patience and precision.

They went to work, moving through protocols that seemed as ritualized as any spell my husband had ever described. I watched them press and probe and examine, knowing it was futile. Walt had already rolled his final save.

When they finally stepped out of the office, confirming what we already knew, I signed their papers, answered questions mechanically, and tried to maintain my composure.

I felt an arm circle my shoulders. It was Brian's. The loud one, rendered silent. His presence was solid, unexpectedly anchoring. The scent of his cinnamon gum, oddly comforting.

"He was happy," Brian said, his voice rough. "You saw his face when we started playing. You gave him that."

Next to us, Kevin stood beside Nate, their shoulders nearly touching. Kevin's posture remained ramrod straight, but his hand rested lightly near Nate's elbow, not quite touching, but available. Understanding without words. Nate stared at the floor, and his fingers worked in that steady rhythm I'd noticed since the airport. The dust he'd scattered still glittered on the table inside.

"I knew it was bad," Kevin said. "But I thought we'd have more time to..."

"Finish the campaign?" I completed his thought.

He nodded, looking ashamed.

"Stories never really finish," I told him, remembering all the nights Walt sat up in bed, notebook in hand, muttering about plot threads and redemption arcs. "They simply reach a point where someone else picks them up."

I walked over to my knitting bag and pulled out a leather-bound journal I'd kept stashed there the past few months. "He knew he was fading fast. Made me write it all down." I opened it to show them. "Every possible path your characters might take. Every secret he planned to reveal."

Their eyes widened at the sight of my cramped handwriting filling the pages.

"He sat there and dictated it to me for weeks, and I did my best to capture it all. This wasn't his finale; it's your next beginning."

Kevin touched the journal reverently. "You're suggesting we continue?"

"He made me promise. No hospitals at the end. No machines. Just home." I gestured to the table in the office with its scattered dice and papers. "You gave him the thing he wanted most."

"Walt knew Eldyrane wasn't his story alone. It was yours. All of yours. And maybe this will give you all a chance to keep going."

"It won't be the same without him," Brian's voice cracked.

"No," I agreed. "It'll be something new. Something that honors what he started." I handed the journal to Kevin, and he held it close to him.

All those Saturdays, they'd been like ghosts drifting through my house. Background characters in Walt's stories about his adventures. The loud one, the precise one, the reserved one with unexpected depths. Now they were there, in voice and grief and flesh, scattered around my living room like characters waiting for direction from a DM who could no longer guide them directly.

They had come for Walt. Crossed miles and comfort zones to be there. Not for closure, but for continuation of what they'd started together. To make sure Walt's story didn't end untold.

There was a light inside that darkest dark that filled me, though: Walt wasn't alone in his final moments. He was in Eldyrane, surrounded by brave and loyal companions. Building worlds until his last breath.

Brian squeezed my shoulder. "We can't let it end like this." His voice was thick with grief.

Nate looked up and met my eyes directly for the first time. "There's still more to do." His words were clear and certain.

Kevin nodded and cradled the journal. "Walt always said the best campaigns write themselves."

I watched something pass between them. An understanding forged through years of shared imagination. I saw it happen—the three of them arriving at a silent agreement.

The party would endure. For Walt. For the story. For each other.

Lay On Hands

Lay On Hands

Nathan flipped through his *Player's Handbook*. The worn binding almost split where he'd opened it countless times to the same page. He'd memorized the paladin class description by now, but he reread it anyway, lips moving silently as his eyes swept over the familiar words: *Divine Sense. Lay on Hands. Divine Smite.*

On his desk, cluttered with paint jars and brushes, sat a meticulously painted Aasimar paladin figurine, its silver armor intricately detailed with tiny celestial symbols, wings spread in preparation for flight. Nathan had spent three evenings just on the seraph wing detailing, layering white and gold until they seemed to glow. He picked up the miniature carefully, turning it in the afternoon light streaming through his bedroom window.

"Nathan?" His mother's voice drifted up from downstairs. "Are you heading out soon?"

He set the paladin down precisely in its spot and glanced at his phone: 2:47 p.m. The group would be setting up their session by now, claiming the big table in the back corner of Grayson's Hobby Shop. Nathan had watched them on enough Saturdays to know their routine. They all went to the same school, but Nathan had never spoken directly to any of them.

"Yeah," he called back, though his voice barely carried beyond his door. He cleared his throat and tried again. "Going now."

Nathan slipped the book into his backpack—not that he'd need it, but holding it made him feel less like he was lurking. He'd discovered the weekly game by accident two months ago, browsing the paint section when their laughter had drawn him toward the gaming tables, a confusing mix of sounds and expressions he could never quite decipher. But the game itself was a language he understood perfectly. Now Saturdays meant finding a nearby shelf to examine while stealing glances at their campaign and feeling the familiar twist in his chest.

The autumn air bit at his cheeks as he walked the six blocks to Grayson's. His hand played a steady rhythm against his thigh: one-two-three, one-two-three—a habit that helped him think.

The bell above the shop door chimed at his arrival. Mr. Grayson looked up from behind the counter and nodded—a wordless greeting they'd established weeks ago. Nathan headed toward the model paints, positioning himself with a clear view of the gaming area.

The other kids were already deep in session. Marcus, the Dungeon Master, sat behind his screen, making dramatic gestures as he described the encounter. The other four players clustered around the table, dice scattered between them like tiny gems. Nathan recognized each of their characters by now: Emma's elegant elf wizard, Jake's armored fighter, Lily's halfling rogue, and...

David's paladin.

Nathan's attention fixed on the unpainted pewter miniature David moved across the battle mat. While the others had gorgeous, customized figures, David's was straight from the package—gray with rough mold lines still visible. The sword had a small chip where David must have dropped it at some point.

"Your turn, David," Marcus said.

David picked up his d20, shook it in cupped hands, and let it roll. "Fifteen! Does that hit?"

"Barely. Roll damage."

As David reached for his damage die, his sleeve caught the edge of his character sheet. Papers scattered, and his little pewter paladin tumbled to the floor.

"Aw, man," David muttered, dropping to his hands and knees to search for it.

Nathan moved before he'd decided to. Three steps brought him to the edge of their table, close enough to see that the miniature had rolled near the shelves. David was looking in the wrong direction, feeling around under the far side of the table.

The gray paladin lay there, forgotten and utterly ordinary.

No hero should be left broken in the darkness. Nathan's hand closed around it.

He straightened, slipped the miniature into his pocket, and walked back toward the paint display. His heart pounded in his ears, but his face remained neutral as he studied a rack of brushes.

"I can't find it anywhere," David announced from under the table, frustration evident in his voice.

"Here, take one of my spares," Emma said, pulling a small case from her bag. "We can look for it after the session."

"Thanks," David replied, and Nathan could hear the disappointment.

Nathan stayed another twenty minutes, long enough not to seem suspicious, then left Grayson's with his usual silent nod to the owner. Outside, his hand found the figure in his pocket. The metal was warm from his body heat, and he could feel the chip in the sword beneath his thumb. A smile tugged at the corners of his mouth as he walked home.

The following Saturday, Nathan stood outside Grayson's for a full five minutes before working up the courage to go inside. Every step toward the shop felt like walking toward the edge of a cliff.

The bell chimed his arrival, and Mr. Grayson looked up with a familiar nod, but something in his expression seemed different—more attentive, perhaps. Nathan's stomach dropped. Did he know?

"There he is!"

The shout came from the gaming section. Nathan's head snapped toward the sound and found all five members of the D&D group staring at him. Jake was pointing directly at him, and David had risen from his chair.

"That's him," David said, his voice carrying across the shop. "The one who took my miniature."

Nathan's legs felt like water. The other customers in the shop turned to look, and Mr. Grayson stepped out from behind the counter. The group was moving toward him now, a semicircle of accusation that made Nathan want to bolt for the door.

"We know you were here last week," Emma said, pointing at Nathan. "And David's paladin went missing right after you were standing by our table."

"Just give it back," Jake added. "We're not going to call the cops or anything."

Nathan's mouth opened, but no words came. His deepest fear surfaced—the reason he never spoke up, never joined conversations, never took risks. His hand found his backpack strap and squeezed.

"Look, we get it," Lily said, her voice gentler than the others. "You want to play. You've been watching us for weeks. But you can't just take our stuff."

"Seriously," David said, "that miniature's not painted or anything. Why would you even want it?"

Nathan's hand worked against his thigh, faster now. The words were there—he could feel them pushing against his teeth—but they felt too big, too risky. What if they didn't understand? What if they laughed?

"Nathan?" Mr. Grayson's voice was gentle but firm. "Do you have something that belongs to these folks?"

Nathan nodded slowly. With trembling hands, he unzipped his backpack and withdrew a tissue-wrapped bundle. The group leaned forward as he carefully peeled away the layers.

The miniature that appeared had been transformed.

David's paladin now wore deep blue armor with silver trim, each plate carefully shaded to show wear and battle damage. The sword gleamed with metallic paint, and Nathan had turned the chip itself into a deliberate notch—a sign of hard-fought battles. But most stunning of all were the great seraph wings that seemed to resonate with light, white feathers edged in gold that caught the shop's fluorescent lighting and made them seem almost real.

"Holy crap," David said.

The others crowded closer. Emma reached out, then stopped herself. "Can I...?"

Nathan nodded and carefully placed the miniature

in her palm. She turned it slowly, examining every angle.

"This is incredible," she breathed. "Look at the detail work. The highlighting on the armor, the highlights in the wings. You did this in a week?"

Nathan just nodded.

"You did this for me?" David asked. "But... why?"

Nathan looked down at his hands. His thumbnail had left small indentations on his index finger from pressure. "It was... incomplete. A paladin should shine with divine light."

"It's cool, I guess." Jake crossed his arms. "But you still stole it, dude."

"Why didn't you just ask to borrow it?" Lily asked, tilting her head.

Nathan pursed his lips and shrugged his shoulders.

The silence stretched for a long moment. Marcus looked at Jake, then at the miniature, and then back to Nathan.

Nathan averted his eyes.

Then Marcus laughed—not mockingly, but with genuine delight.

"So, you've been watching us for weeks because you wanted to play?"

Nathan nodded again.

"And instead of just asking, you took David's mini and spent a week painting it because you thought it deserved to be beautiful?"

Another nod.

"That's the most hardcore way anyone has ever asked to join our game," Marcus said, still laughing.

Emma handed the figure back to David, who held it as if it were made of spun glass. "Thanks," he whispered.

"You know," Lily said, "we actually need a fifth. We've been talking about it for a while."

Nathan's head snapped up. "R-really?"

"Really," Marcus confirmed. "You're here every week anyway." He gestured toward the gaming area, where their books and dice still waited. "Are you interested?"

Nathan looked at their faces—no longer accusatory, but welcoming. Hopeful, even. His backpack held his own painted miniatures, his dice, and his carefully studied character sheets. All the pieces he'd need to no longer stand on the sidelines. To belong to something.

"Yes," Nathan said, and for the first time in weeks, his voice didn't shake. "I'd like that."

David grinned and held up his transformed paladin. "Well, then, let's go save the world."

About the Author

Ric Perrott has spent his life telling stories. First as excuses to his mother, then in lines of code, and now with words on the page. A lifelong gamer, musician, voracious reader, and sometime screenwriter—he decided it was time to let the dice roll and share the stories that have been roaming through his imagination for decades. *Pick Up the Pieces* is his first published short story.

Ric lives in Florida with his family, far too many books, and a wellspring of unfinished ideas. His debut novel, "The Family" will be published in December 2025.

www.ingramcontent.com/pod-product-compliance
Lightning Source LLC
Chambersburg PA
CBHW050500110726
47899CB00003B/1019